Contents

Great Moments

Figure skating. It's popular and thrilling, it's "all or nothing." A skater has just a few minutes to skate her best — land all her jumps and spin to perfection — and there's no starting over. But some skaters rise above all the pressure and create those memorable moments that thrill fans forever.

Kurt Browning

1996 Canadian Pro Championships

After a rocky start to his pro skating career, Kurt Browning finds his groove and triumphs with a brilliant skate. He nails all his triples and pours his soul into an unforgettable performance.

Jayne Torvill & Christopher Dean

1984 Olympic Games

Captivating audiences around the world, ice dancers Jayne Torvill and Christopher Dean win Olympic gold with nine perfect scores of 6.0, the highest number of sixes ever achieved by any skaters.

★ FIGURE SKATING STARS ★ TIPS ★ FACTS ★

Magic on Ice

★ ★ ★ ★ PATTY CRANSTON ★ ★ ★ ★

Kids Can Press

To Ashleigh, Robert, Michael (and Kimmee)

The author's name is the only one to appear on the front of this book but there are so many other people who devoted their time and expertise to its completion. My sincerest appreciation goes to the following:

Laura Barry; Valerie Bartlett; Andrea Bolla; Jake and Rene Brunott; Robert Burk and students Mary-Helen French and Rachel Ouellette; Ellen and Petra Burka; Frank Carroll; Marcus Christensen; Osborne Colson; Toller Cranston; Diane Crites; Cathy Dalton; David D'Cruz; Courtney and Donna Evans; Janet Fournier of Healthy, Happy and Fit; Laura Hallis and Michael Otter of the Figure Skating Boutique; Doug Haw; Thom Hayim; Carol Heiss-Jenkins; Debbie Islam; Brian Klavano, Cindy Lang and Laurie Vlandis of Ice Castle International Training Center; Doug and Michelle Leigh; Kerry Leitch; Olga Litvinchuk; Shelley MacLeod; Paul Martini; Brian Orser; Crispin Redhead; Astrid Shrubb; Allan Stewart of Canada's Sports Hall of Fame; Barbara Underhill; Tracy Wilson; and Marina Zueva.

Special thanks also to Kids Can Press publishers, Valerie Hussey and Ricky Englander, who encouraged me to write skating books; designer, Julia Naimska for making this book look so great; and editor, Liz MacLeod, not only for her guidance and advice but her perpetual good cheer.

And my heartfelt thanks to the one who's always there for me, Bob Cranston, my husband and best friend.

Text copyright © 1998 by Patty Cranston

We acknowledge the support of the Canada Council for the Arts and the Ontario Arts Council for our publishing program.

Published in Canada by
Kids Can Press Ltd.
29 Birch Avenue
Toronto, ON M4V 1E2

Published in the U.S. by
Kids Can Press Ltd.
85 River Rock Drive, Suite 202
Buffalo, NY 14207

Edited by Elizabeth MacLeod
Designed by Julia Naimska
Printed in Hong Kong by Wing King Tong Co. Ltd.

CM 98 0 9 8 7 6 5 4 3 2 1

Canadian Cataloging in Publication Data

Cranston, Patty
Magic on ice: figure skating stars, tips and facts

Includes index.
ISBN 1-55074-455-0

1. Skating — Juvenile literature. I. Title.

GV850.4.C72 1998   j796.91'2   C98-930466-3

Photo credits
Andrea Bolla Collection: 27 (top and bottom right). **Petra Burka Collection:** 6 (left), 8 (both). **Dick Button Personal Collection:** 7 (top). **Canada's Sports Hall of Fame:** 7 (bottom). **Paul Harvath:** 14 (right), 37 (left). **Thom Hayim Photography:** 6 (right), 14 (left), 15 (top left), 16 (both), 17 (top left and right), 20 (all), 21 (all), 22 (all), 23 (all), 26 (both), 27 (left), 28 (bottom), 32 (right). **Holiday Studio:** 24 (left). **Heinz Kluetmeier:** 35 (right). **Cindy Lang:** 33 (right). **Stephan Potopnyk:** cover (middle), 3 (top), 4 (both), 5 (left, right), 10, 11 (top right), 12/13 (all), 24 (right), 25 (both), 29 (bottom), 30 (both), 31 (middle), 32 (left), 33 (left), 36, 37 (middle), back cover (top and middle left, bottom right). **Dino Ricci:** 9 (right), 17 (bottom right), 18 (right), 19 (left), 28 (top), 29 (top), 37 (right). **Cam Silverson:** cover (top and bottom left, top and bottom right), 3 (bottom), 5 (middle), 11 (top and bottom left, bottom right), 15 (bottom left, right), 18 (left), 19 (right), 29 (middle), 31 (left), 34 (right), 38 (both), 39 (all), 40 (both), 41 (both), 42, 43 (both), 44 (both), 45 (both), 46 (both), 47 (both), back cover (bottom left, top and middle right). **Margaret S. Williamson:** 9 (left, middle). **Tracy Wilson Collection:** 3 (middle), 31 (right), 34 (left), 35 (top and bottom left).

Tara Lipinski

1998 Olympic Games

Her goal in 1998 was to enjoy the entire Olympic experience and perform her best. But Tara Lipinski skates away with the gold medal when she performs with energy and confidence to become the youngest skater ever to win the Olympics.

Kristi Yamaguchi

1992 Olympic Games

The 1992 Olympic women's event was set to be the battle of the triple axel. While her main competitors crash and burn, Kristi Yamaguchi earns the top prize, thanks to her famous consistency.

Elvis Stojko

1997 World Championships

In fourth position after the short program, Elvis Stojko is almost out of contention. The gutsy Stojko skates flawlessly and uncorks a perfect quad-toe, triple-toe combination — the first-ever in Worlds — to win the gold medal.

How It All Began

It's amazing to think that hundreds of years ago in some parts of Europe you probably could have skated to school in the winter. The canals froze into huge outdoor roadways and lakes became skating rinks.

Sound like fun? That's because your skates are probably sturdy and fit you well. But skates weren't always as snug as yours. Some of the very first blades were carved out of animal bones and, like the heavy wooden blades used later, tied around skaters' winter boots with thick straps. Iron blades came next and were better than wooden ones because they allowed skaters to carve and grip the ice.

Iron blades were a huge improvement, but skaters couldn't perform "tricks" (what today's skaters call jumps, spins and other elements) until the 1850s, when an American invented steel blades. They were stronger than blades of iron and much sharper. As well, steel blades can be sharpened so they have what are known as inside and outside edges and allow skaters to perform tricks without slipping.

Skaters used wooden blades less than 200 years ago. Today's steel blades allow skaters to skate on the edges of the blades, which carve out curves (patterns) on the ice. The bigger the curve, the "deeper" the edge. Skaters only use the "flat" (the hollow center part of the blade between the two edges) to change from one edge to the other.

6

American Dick Button was a five-time World Champion who won Olympics twice, in 1948 and 1952.

With better equipment, skaters invented jumps and other moves and wanted to experience the thrill of competition. At the first World Championships, held in 1896, only men took part. When British skater Madge Syers competed against the men in 1902 and almost beat champ Ulrich Salchow, women were quickly banned from men's events. Separate events for women were first held in 1906.

Norwegian Sonja Henie was one of the first superstars of the sport. Between 1927 and 1936 she won three Olympic gold medals and ten World Championships, more than any other female skater. While other women wore black skates, Henie wore flesh-tone ones. Other skaters imitated her, so Henie changed to white skates, the most popular color today.

By the time steel blades were in use, skaters' blades were attached to boots that were specially developed for skating. They laced up tightly and had more support than ordinary boots. As well, the blades couldn't shift around like their earlier, strapped-on versions, so skaters felt more secure.

Olympic and World Champion Barbara Ann Scott was European Champion in 1947 and 1948. North Americans weren't allowed to compete at the European Championships after this Canadian won. Scott was also the first North American to win a World title.

Europeans were the best figure skaters until the bombs of World War II destroyed many of the ice rinks and sent Europe's best coaches to North America in search of jobs. Today figure skating is popular all over the world and superstar skaters come from many countries.

Competitions Then and Now

Many people think that today's skaters face far more pressure than yesterday's stars because of the constant media attention and the demand for difficult tricks. But older skaters dealt with outdoor conditions such as wind, rain, snow and freezing-cold temperatures.

"I had to skate half in the sun and half in the shade, so the sunny ice was mushy and slow and the shady ice was hard and fast," says Petra Burka (left) about conditions at the 1966 World Championships. "When the men skated there was a raging snowstorm," this Canadian and World Champion continues. "The Zamboni broke down in the middle of the rink, and the ice was covered in snow but couldn't be cleaned."

Check out the costumes of this mid-1960s Canadian figure skating team. Burka is seventh from the left.

Since the last outdoor Worlds were held in 1967, skaters no longer worry about the weather. And they no longer skate the difficult technical moves known as compulsory figures, which were dropped from World competition in 1990.

American Janet Lynn was often the best freeskater in the world but struggled with her figures. She would have been the 1972 Olympic Champion instead of the bronze medalist, if figures hadn't been included in the competition.

Facts on Figures

Skaters used to devote more than half their practice time to figures — variations on a number eight. There were about 75 figures that a skater practiced during his career — some with two circles and others with three. Some figures, such as "rockers," involved turning from front to back or vice versa, while for others, skaters made a circle within a circle.

Skaters performed figures on one foot at a time, making as perfect circles as possible. They had to make either three or six "tracings," depending on the figure. Judges examined the tracings (carvings) and based their marks on these, as well as on the skater's form and posture.

In the past, a poor freeskater could win a competition if he had a good lead after figures.

Today's skaters, such as Kurt Browning (below) know that the ice conditions, sound system and dressing rooms will be perfect, but like it or not, they always have TV cameras in their face. It's a part of competition life, and so is dealing with enthusiastic fans.

Tricks of the Trade

When you watch skating on TV and hear the announcers talk about axels and lutzes; quadruple toe, triple toes; and flying camels do you feel confused? So many tricks — jumps, spins and other elements — look the same. But not to skaters!

There are six main jumps: salchow, toe-loop (usually referred to as a "toe"), loop, flip, lutz and axel. Each of these jumps can be performed as singles, doubles, triples or quadruples. Skaters learn the single jumps first. All of them, except the axel, begin with the skater moving backward and rotating once in the air before landing backward. The axel takes off forward but still lands backward and, as a result, includes an extra half turn in the air.

A skater uses her toe pick for the take-off of the toe, flip and lutz jumps, while she uses an inside or outside edge for the other jumps. Once a skater masters all the single jumps, she's ready for doubles. Then the best skaters try triples, and finally, quads.

Skaters can perform a number of jumps in a row (in combination), as in a triple axel, triple toe. Judges give skaters better marks for combinations because they're a lot harder to land than one jump by itself.

Pairs skaters combine jumps and spins in unison with lifts, throws and field moves. Here, Isabelle Brasseur and Lloyd Eisler show their majestic form in an overhead lift.

A top skater has to have more than great jumps. She must also learn the basic spins: the scratch spin, sit spin, camel, flying camel, layback and death drop. Usually only women perform the layback spin, which requires a flexible back, while men are more suited to the death drop — a high-flying jumping spin in which the skater drops from an in-air position parallel to the ice right down into a sit spin.

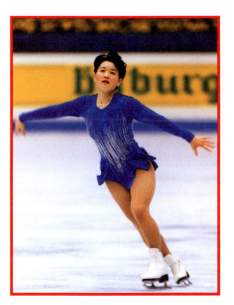

Among the women on the pro circuit, 1994 World Champion Yuka Sato's feet are the fastest-moving with quick steps, turns and edges that she strings together in what's called footwork.

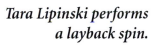

Tara Lipinski performs a layback spin.

Isabelle and Paul Duchesnay pushed the limits and rules of ice dancing with their bold and innovative programs.

Moves such as Rudy Galindo's Ina Bauer fill spaces between tricks.

Precision Team Skating

If you love skating and like being part of a team, then precision team skating is for you. Instead of skating alone, you get to share the fun of practicing and competing with other team members. There's a precision team for everyone, no matter what your age or skill level.

Junior and senior level competitive precision teams skate both a long and short program. There are five required elements for the short program: the circle, line, pinwheel, block (above) and intersection.

In this line, skaters travel in a straight line from one end of the rink to the other.

You don't have to be a top skater to be in precision, but you should have good skating skills and be prepared to practice as often as every day. You also need a natural instinct to keep your lines straight. Skaters on the best teams don't have to use their eyes to do this — they feel the tension in the line from skater to skater.

Elite team members devote many hours to their on- and off-ice training. Off the ice, their physical training concentrates on building muscle strength and aerobic endurance. The team also practices its routines on the floor without skates so that skaters can work on the unison of their head and arm movements. Mental training focuses on handling competition pressure.

One of the things precision skaters love about their sport is the speed they build up as they race down the ice. It's that speed that also makes precision thrilling for audiences. Skating so fast can be fun but it can also be dangerous. Most precision skaters say that the worst part of team skating is if you trip and pull other skaters down with you. But as Cathy Dalton — coach of *black ice,* winners of the 1997 World Challenge Cup Championship — says, "It's a team effort. You skate together and you win and lose together."

When skating the circle, precision skaters must perform footwork as well as make a "hand-hold change," that is, switch the way they're holding hands.

Did You Know?

... the youngest Olympic competitor ever was 11 years old? British skater Cecilia Colledge took part in the 1932 games and was also the first skater to land a double jump in women's competition.

... at one time skaters were not allowed to raise their arms above the waist? Coach Gus Lussi helped change that rule, insisting that skaters needed their arms to spin and to launch their jumps.

... most ice dancers use skate blades (below, bottom) that are about 2.5 cm (1 in.) shorter in the heel than other skaters' blades (below, top)? Dancers' blades are shorter so they won't trip when they do footwork.

... Olympic and World Champion Peggy Fleming (above) pinned a gum wrapper to her dress for luck before winning the 1968 Olympics?

... it's important that girls learn triple jumps before puberty, when they tend to have less fear? Boys learn triples more easily after puberty, when their bodies are stronger and they seem to have more courage.

... most top skaters need at least two pairs of skates each year? The skates are usually custom-made. Skaters dread breaking in new skates since they are very stiff and cause blisters.

... sometimes a skater learns a new jump with the aid of a jumping harness? It fits around the skater's waist and is attached to a pulley. The coach pulls on a cord to raise the skater into the air and rotate her the correct way for the jump.

... spins are much more tiring than jumps? That's why skaters perform the longest and most difficult spins at the end of their program, after the toughest jumps are out of the way. Here Todd Eldredge performs a corkscrew spin.

... at each major competition, skaters participate in a "draw" to determine the order in which they'll skate? One by one they select a number from a hat. Skaters perform in groups of six and most prefer not to skate in first or sixth place. The ice is resurfaced after every two groups so that it never gets too "chopped up" with ruts and gouges.

... skating a long program is like running a sprint for $4\frac{1}{2}$ minutes with hurdles thrown in as well?

... Elvis Stojko, shown here with Kurt Browning, always ties up his left skate first?

Skate Talk

Your skates are your most important piece of equipment. Here are some tips to remember when you choose your next pair.

Your skates should fit snugly — a little tighter than your running shoes — but you should still be able to wiggle your toes slightly. Don't buy skates that are too big for you hoping that they'll last an extra season. And don't pad them with extra socks — that'll make your feet colder. Air needs to circulate around your feet to keep them warm and it can't if there isn't enough room.

Think about buying a well-made pair of secondhand skates that have good ankle support. How can you tell if they'll give you good support? Try bending the skate's upper part: if it bends easily, there's not much support left. Molded plastic skates may feel strong, but avoid buying them, because they're rigid and impossible to break in.

Skates aren't the only important equipment for a skater. If you're a beginner you should always wear a proper-fitting helmet. And wear layers of comfortable, loose clothes so you can peel them off. At cold rinks, keep warm with a jacket and snow pants.

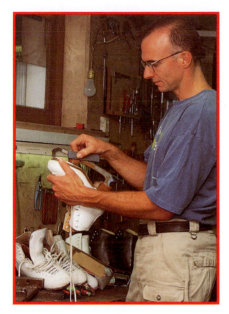

Sharpen your blades at the beginning of the season and regularly after that. If you slip when you skate, you probably need a sharpening.

If your new skates give you blisters, pad your ankle bones. Take round cosmetic sponges (buy them at a drugstore), rip a circle about 2.5 cm (1 in.) in diameter out of the middle of each one and place a ring around each ankle bone before you put on your skates.

Some skaters pull their laces really tight, but that can cut off the blood circulation to your feet. If your skates give you good support, you need only tie them securely.

After skating, wipe your blades dry with a towel or soft cloth. For added protection, make a "towel bag" for each skate. It's easy: take two old bath towels, fold one in half, sew up the two opposite sides, and insert a skate in the open side. Repeat with the other towel.

Skate guards are used to walk to and from the ice surface. Don't put them on just after you've dried your blades, because the blades still hold some moisture and the skate guards will cause them to rust.

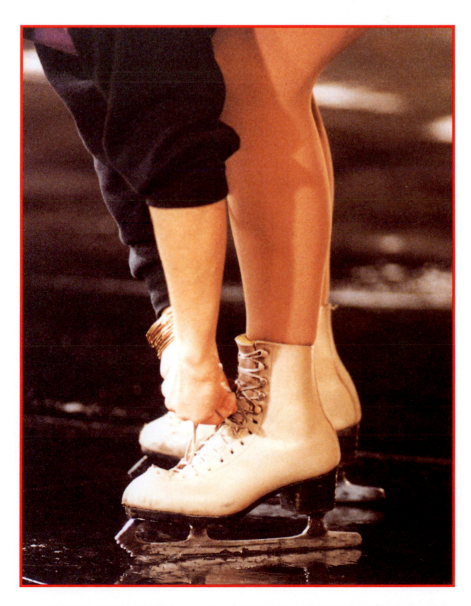

What Does ★ That Mean?

Does it sometimes seem as if figure skaters, their coaches and commentators are speaking a secret language? Here are translations of some of the most commonly used phrases.

Caught an Edge: A skater falters or falls because his blade catches in a rut.

Compulsory Dances, Original Dance (OD), Free Dance: The three elements that make up the ice dance competition. Every team skates the same compulsory dances to the same pattern, steps and music. Each team chooses its own music and choreography for the OD as well as for the free dance. The OD is based on a ballroom dance, such as the tango, which Shae-Lynn Bourne and Victor Kraatz demonstrate (left). The free dance is four minutes long and includes original choreography.

Deep Edges: When a skater really uses the edges of his blades to carve and grip the ice. Skating with deep edges allows a skater to skate at a sharp angle to the ice. It earns high marks since it requires more control and strength, and better technique than shallow edges.

Field Moves: Elements such as the spiral, Ina Bauer and spread eagle — performed here by Brian Boitano. Good skaters will cover a lot of ice when performing these moves.

Flow: The smoothness and grace that skaters show as they move from element to element and interpret their programs to music.

Footwork: A series of steps. It includes turns, twists, hops and lunges and is completed in a circle, straight line or S-shaped formation.

Nailed It: When a skater lands a perfect jump or a pairs team completes a perfect throw, as Elena Berezhnaia and Anton Sikharulidze are about to do here.

Choreography

A skater may spend hours listening to music with his choreographer and/or coach to choose a piece that motivates him and suits his skating style. The choreographer ensures that the skater interprets the music suitably and the program is "well laid out," which means it uses all parts of the ice, the jumps are well spaced, and the skater moves in different directions.

In the photo above, Christine Hough (left) and Kurt Browning discuss how to interpret their music with choreographer Sandra Bezic.

Popped It: When a skater completes a single jump instead of the planned triple or double.

Short and Long Programs: A skater's or pairs' short program is approximately $2\frac{1}{2}$ minutes long and contains certain required elements — jumps, spins, footwork and field moves for singles, and for pairs, those elements as well as lifts, throws and pairs' spins. The long program consists of the skater's choice of elements, including a variety of tricks and original choreography. The men's and pairs' long program is $4\frac{1}{2}$ minutes long and the women's is 4 minutes long.

Off-Ice Training

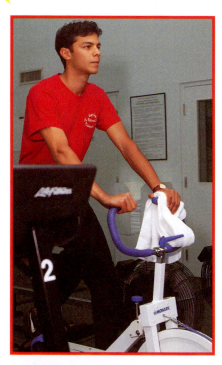

If you want to be a better skater, think about adding off-ice exercises to your training. Stretching can improve your flexibility, and cardiovascular conditioning will increase your endurance. Classes in dance, such as ballet and jazz, as well as drama lessons will help you achieve the grace and poise of a top skater.

If you can't make time for off-ice workouts, at least try to warm up before each practice. Take ten minutes to skip, bike, jog, run, or climb stairs until you break a sweat. Then you're ready for some easy pre-skate stretches — see the photos.

Stretch to music whenever possible. It's fun and will help you practice moving to a beat. Hold your stretches for at least 20 seconds and breathe deeply. When you exhale, gently push the stretch further. Here are some important muscle groups to limber up before skating. Always start on one side and repeat each stretch on the other side.

Groin: Sit on the floor and bend both legs so that your feet are flat and together. Grab your ankles, keep your back straight and gently push your upper legs toward the floor with your elbows.

Hamstrings: Sit on the floor with both legs straight. Use your hands to grab both ankles and pull your upper body forward as far as possible. If you can't keep your legs straight, flex your knees slightly.

Quadriceps (Quads): Lie on the floor on your stomach, grab the front of your right ankle and, without pulling back on the foot or letting your knees separate, pull the right leg back until your heel touches your buttocks.

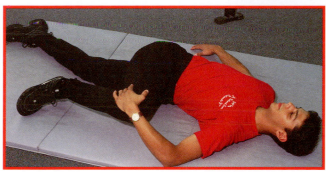

Lower Back: Lie on your back, bend your right knee and gently pull it over to your left side, keeping your right arm and shoulder flat on the floor.

Hip Flexors: Grab your left leg as shown and pull it toward your chest. Push your lower back into the floor to feel a stretch in your right hip flexor.

Being physically fit isn't all you need to skate well. Mental training is also important. It helps you develop confidence and a positive attitude. Many successful athletes regularly use a technique called visualization to achieve these qualities. Give it a try: close your eyes and imagine doing a new trick perfectly. Or watch another skater who's perfected the skill and imagine doing it just as well.

In this skaters' dance class, instructor Crispin Redhead demonstrates correct off-ice form.

Get Skating

Your off-ice warm-up is complete and you're ready to skate. Structure your session to include an on-ice warm-up, skills practice and a cooldown. Try working on new skills with a friend or in a small group.

Stroking is the best warm-up and conditioning exercise on the ice. It builds cardiovascular endurance and stamina, and strengthens a skater's leg muscles, her most important muscles. Just skate forward along the length of the rink and do crosscuts (crossovers) around the ends. (If you can't do these, just keep skating forward.) Repeat for a few laps in both directions without stopping and then try the same exercise skating backward. Stroke for at least 5 minutes at first and try to build up to 15 minutes.

If you're tall enough, you can practice your spiral position by lifting one leg on top of the boards and holding it there (for stretch). Then take your leg off the boards (below) and still hold it up (for strength). You can also do this facing the boards and have a partner lift your leg. Or do it at home, using the kitchen counter instead of the arena boards.

To learn a spread eagle (see page 18) you have to practice your "turn-out." Next time you're at the rink, face the boards, hold on to them and turn your feet out, heel to heel, in opposite directions (left). Then push your hips forward against the boards and hold this position. If your knees hurt, bend them slightly.

Interval Training

To improve your conditioning, try interval training. Skate forward or backward without stopping for three minutes. Push yourself hard enough so that your heart rate stays up — that's when you're too out of breath to talk. Rest for three minutes and then repeat this exercise twice. You can do this alone, but it's more fun if you do it in a group.

Cool Down

At the end of a session, you need to lower your heart rate and extend and stretch your leg muscles. Stroke slowly and deliberately around the rink, making sure that your legs and arms are fully extended with each movement. Repeat for a few laps. Then practice your spiral first on the right foot, then the left.

If you have time during your cooldown, try double sculling, a good stretch-and-strength exercise for the groin and inner quads. Starting with your feet

together, make wide semi-circles with each foot and pull the feet back in together. Repeat several times down the length of the rink.

Meet a Judge: Debbie Islam

Islam shows the grace and form that made her a former Junior Canadian Champion.

One of a judge's main tasks is to guide competitive skaters. Here, Islam goes through her checklist with Canadian Olympic team member Jeffrey Langdon to make sure he is including all his elements.

Have you ever wondered how it feels to watch a skater perform and then assign him a mark? Debbie Islam — a former international competitor — does just that when she judges competitions. Here's the scoop on what it's like to be in the hot seat at competition.

Why did you become a judge?
Judging presented a challenge for me. It also gives me an opportunity to stay involved in skating.

Do you have to pass tests to be a judge?
Definitely! We have extensive training at seminars, then we have to write exams for each test and competitive level.

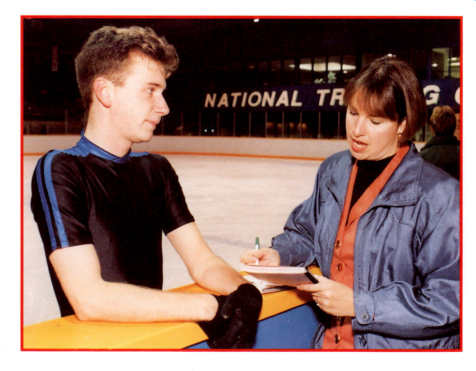

How do you prepare for judging a competition?

The main thing judges do is attend the skaters' practices. We make sure they're doing their elements and programs according to the rules and we look at the standard of skating. This gives us an idea of what the marks might be on competition day. I carry my rule book with me all the time so I can keep up with constant rule changes.

What are you looking for when you judge a skater?

Judges give marks in two areas. The technical merit mark is given for the difficulty and quality of the jumps, spins and footwork. The presentation mark judges choreography, whether the skater uses all parts of the ice, if he varies the direction in which he skates, and how well he interprets the music.

How does it feel to sit in the judge's seat?

Often I wish I was back on the ice myself. I get so nervous knowing that I can't control what happens on the ice. It's difficult to see a good skater "bomb," but it's my duty to judge the performance I see that day. On the other hand, when I watch a spectacular skate, I wish I could go wild with the crowd but I have to focus on my job.

What do you like best about judging?

Judging is my connection to skating and the lifelong friends I've made. As part of the team, you feel so proud to represent your country.

What do you like least about judging?

Judges deal with intense media criticism. To mark a skater, judges have to make split-second decisions but still remember the rules. Few fans realize how technical skating is.

What was your best moment in judging?

The first time I gave a six to Brian Orser. He skated incredibly, and I thought, "I'm going to do it." The next best moment was awarding Elvis Stojko a six after he nailed his quad-triple.

At international competitions, Islam (in red) is one of seven or nine judges.

Competition Day

My name is Andrea, I'm 15, and I skate six days a week. When a competition day arrives I have a special routine that I follow. Even if my competition isn't until the evening, I start getting ready the night before as I'm going to sleep. I close my eyes and imagine skating perfectly. When I wake up the next morning, here's how I prepare.

8:00 A.M.

I shower, get on my warm-up suit and have breakfast: fruit, hot oatmeal and orange juice. I polish my skates, then gather my music tapes — I take two in case one breaks — and a blank video so that I can get a copy of my performance.

9:30 A.M.

Time to head to the rink, where I register at the competitors' desk and hand in my cassettes. In the change room I eat a banana and drink some water. With my skates in hand, I find a quiet place to warm up. Then I lace up my skates, always the right foot first for good luck.

11:30 A.M.

During practice I try to stay focused. "Be confident and breathe," I tell myself. Even when I make mistakes, I pretend that I am skating my best. Back in the dressing room, I take off my skates, dry my blades, and leave for home.

1:15 P.M.

Lunch: I have pasta with low-fat sauce so I'll have lots of energy without feeling full. After lunch I take a nap and then a short walk.

4:15 P.M.

I put on my makeup, fix my hair in a bun and then shake my head to make sure the hair pins stay in place. Then I have a snack: a bagel, an orange and herbal tea. Next, I pin onto my dress a "Guardian Angel," my good luck charm. "Pack an extra pair of skate laces and another costume," I remind myself, "just in case."

5:30 P.M.

I arrive at the rink an hour early and try to stay calm. I visualize performing my routine perfectly and breathe deeply. After my off-ice warm-up and stretches, I put on my skates.

6:30 P.M.

All the competitors get six minutes to warm up, which is just enough time to practice my tricks. Off the ice I pace the hall until it's my turn to skate. I tuck in my laces, and sip water so my mouth won't get dry.

6:45 P.M.

My name is called and I glide to center ice, keeping my chin up so that I feel confident. As I perform, I concentrate and take one trick at a time.

7:00 P.M.

Whew! It's over! I can relax and watch the rest of my competitors. After my event's over, I run to the results board to check the standings. I can't believe it — my name's at the top — I won!

The Road to the Top

It takes years to become a top skater and getting there requires incredible commitment and talent. It also takes determination, discipline and sacrifice.

Katarina Witt is known as one of the world's toughest competitors. She has a remarkable record — Witt has topped the podium at an incredible two Olympics and four World Championships.

The road from beginner to champion starts the same way for everyone: learning to stand on skates. Next come group lessons. At this level most kids skate once or twice a week, but as they progress past beginner classes they may skate several days a week. Top skaters may show some early talent, but more likely they progress because they love to skate and thrive under the pressure of competition.

The most dedicated skaters take private lessons so they can compete and try tests. Even some of the youngest competitors train two or three hours a day, five days a week for about ten months a year.

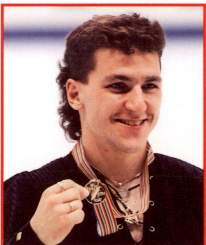

Touring with the Pros

Skaters who make it to the top often have exciting careers ahead of them touring with other professional skaters. They become great friends with the skaters on tour and get to travel all over the world. They may also finally earn enough to pay back the money they spent on costumes, ice time, coaching and other training.

The skaters no longer have to train for hours every day, but their schedules are still hectic and very demanding. For instance, the skaters may arrive in a city one day, practice, perform in the show that night, then leave the next day and repeat it all over again in the next city. Their schedules also include press conferences, TV shows and radio interviews.

It can be lonely skating your way to the top. Training with the best coaches may mean moving far away from home. As well, the best skaters have little time for activities outside of skating because their schedules juggle on-ice practices with off-ice physical and mental training. Younger elite skaters who travel constantly can't attend regular school, so they also have to cram in time for tutors.

In addition to her family, a top skater has a support team that includes her coach, choreographer, trainer and sports psychologist, as well as experts in nutrition, costumes, music, makeup and hair.

Skating may be serious business but there's always time to have fun.

How Do They Do That?

Biellmann Spin

World champion Denise Biellmann started practicing her trademark spin when she was 11 and her hands have the calluses to prove it.

First she arches her back and reaches over her shoulder for her skate blade. (This puts great strain on her back, shoulder and upper arm.) Once Biellmann has the blade firmly in one hand, she grabs it with the second hand as well and then pulls her foot high over her head.

The Axel

Brian Orser's triple axel is one of the best in the world. In fact, he became the first man to land two triple axels in the same program in competition. After soaring through $3\frac{1}{2}$ revolutions, Orser seems to hang in the air before landing.

Before Orser learned how to perform a triple axel, however, he mastered a single. Here's how he does it: First he lines up his left shoulder, hip and leg so that they're stacked on top of each other on the back outside edge of his skate. When Orser steps forward into the axel, he focuses his eyes on the spot in the air to which he wants the jump to climb. He takes a giant step into the air and rotates $1\frac{1}{2}$ times before landing backward.

Death Spiral

The death spiral is one of the most beautiful pairs moves. The most common ones are the back outside, the back inside and the forward inside death spirals. World Champion Paul Martini — who with partner Barb Underhill has one of the best death spirals — describes how to do a back outside death spiral:

"The partners begin by skating backward, hand to hand. They move quickly over the ice to pick up lots of speed. Then the woman arches her back and leans toward her partner as he makes a pivot — a circle that gets smaller and smaller. This creates a force between the skaters that helps pull the woman down toward the ice. The woman must skate securely on her edge so she doesn't slip, and her body should look evenly arched from skate to head. The pair tries to complete one full circle when they hit their death spiral position."

You may think that during a death spiral the woman's head touches the ice to help her balance. But pairs skaters say that if they used their heads to help perform this move, their heads would be very sore afterwards!

Backflip

You won't see backflips performed at competitions, but skaters still do them in shows. It takes guts to learn a backflip, and Elvis Stojko and coach Doug Leigh can tell you how not to learn it. In a freak accident, Stojko's blade punctured Leigh's forehead, went through his nose — just missed his eye — and cut his chest, requiring 25 stitches. "Safety was not in place," admits Leigh. "Elvis was in a safety harness but I had no protection. So the next day at the rink, in typical Elvis humor, he brought me his motorcross safety equipment to wear: a helmet and chest protector!"

In the photo above, Brian Orser and Scott Hamilton show the right way to perform backflips.

Underhill and Martini demonstrate their excellent form entering a back outside death spiral (above), while Marina Eltsova and Andrei Bushkov (below) perform a forward inside death spiral.

What Coaches Look for

A coach can help you improve your skating but he can't predict how well you'll succeed. So much is up to you. The right attitude is a good start. It means that you arrive on time for lessons, you work hard, you pay attention to your coach and you're enthusiastic. Most coaches will tell you that talent is not as important as grit — the drive to keep training day after day, through the good and bad. Here's what else some of today's top skating coaches think is important.

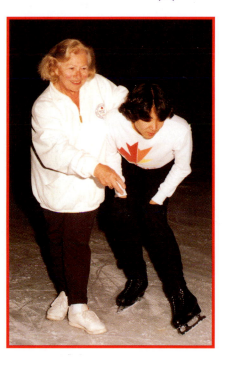

Ellen Burka

Coach of World and Olympic skaters, including Petra Burka and Toller Cranston

"The beginner must have speed, as well as good spring for jumps. A top skater must be low-key, yet have nerves of steel to perform under pressure. Those who win are dedicated and disciplined and are willing to do whatever it takes to succeed."

Doug Leigh

Elvis Stojko's and Brian Orser's coach

"Flair. I look for eye contact and energy. Young kids with potential have that immediately. They're spontaneous, and if you listen to them, you'll hear what their vision is. The top competitor has a no-nonsense attitude and won't accept less than the best from himself."

Kerry Leitch

Coach of World and Olympic pairs teams such as Christine Hough and Doug Ladret

"I look for the ABCs: awareness, balance and coordination. Skaters must be aware of themselves and other skaters on the ice. They must have good balance, coordination, and the courage to perform in competition — and of course, discipline, drive and determination."

Marina Zueva

Gordeeva and Grinkov's coach and choreographer

"I like to work with a disciplined skater who's easy to train. Talent is necessary but hard work is more important. The skater should be small but strong, and have good coordination."

Frank Carroll

Michelle Kwan's coach

"A skater must have the right body, because it's her most important piece of equipment. In young skaters, you look for natural spring and quick twitch muscles (which help a skater rotate quickly in the air during jumps). For the elite skater, discipline and desire are first, talent is second."

Carol Heiss-Jenkins

Olympic and World Champion; coach of international skaters such as Tonia Kwiatkowski

"A skater must be motivated and love the sport with a passion. With passion comes perseverance and discipline: you won't give up when things are going badly. A coach can motivate only if the skater wants to do it."

From Blades to Microphone

You've probably often seen Tracy Wilson on CBS Television commentating at major figure skating competitions. But before Wilson became an announcer, she and her partner Rob McCall won seven Canadian ice dance titles as well as bronze medals in the Olympics and two World Championships. After Wilson retired from skating, TV commentating seemed like the perfect way to stay involved with the sport she loves.

Wilson and McCall were audience favorites who loved to perform.

Why did you become an announcer?

I love skating and I love to talk, and the two go well together.

What training did you take for your job?

When I was skating I took courses to develop my public-speaking skills. I also gave motivational speeches to various businesses and talks for the Canadian World figure skating team.

What do you like most about your job?

I get to travel, talk about skating and maintain my friendships with the skaters.

What's the worst part of your job?

It's awful when I'm talking and I don't know the microphone is on. Or when I lose my concentration and my mind goes blank. Instead of focusing on what I'm saying, I'm thinking, "Uh-oh, I'm on national TV."

Do you get nervous?

Yes, but working with Vern Lundquist and Scott Hamilton helps me relax because they make me laugh. Scott will often tell a joke just as I'm ready to go on-camera.

What surprised you most about your job?

The huge amount of research and preparation involved. Also, it's tough knowing how much to talk as a skater performs. My job's to inform and educate the viewers — explain the tricks, the music and choreography — and not irritate them with too much chatter.

How do you prepare for an event?

First I read material that the research staff has compiled on the skaters. Then I watch them practice, chat with them and, more important, I talk to their coaches. Often a skater's too nervous about the competition and tells me, "Everything's fine. I just want to skate well." But it's the coach who sets the record straight: "We just want to land that first jump and then we're in business."

On the job, Wilson interviews many of the top figure skaters, including 1992 Olympic Champion Victor Petrenko.

Vern Lundquist, Tracy Wilson and Scott Hamilton (left to right), make up the CBS skating broadcast team.

Wilson shares a laugh with (left to right) Kurt Browning, Katarina Witt and Oksana Baiul.

Legends of Figure Skating

Jayne Torvill & Christopher Dean

Great Britain

Olympic Champions, 1984
Olympic Bronze, 1994
World Champions, 1981-1984

Few skaters work harder than ice dancers Jayne Torvill and Christopher Dean. They often practice the same move up to 1000 times! More than a decade after their stunning Olympic victory, they keep improving. Incredibly, Torvill and Dean's third-place finish at the 1994 Olympics was their lowest since 1980, and they've won every other competition they've entered since then.

"If you go back through time you come across some champions who have added to their sport and others who have just been the best of that year. Jayne and Christopher added to the sport."

BETTY CALLAWAY, 1995
Torvill and Dean's coach

Dorothy Hamill

U.S.A.

Olympic Champion, 1976
World Champion, 1976

Dorothy Hamill combined athletic ability and grace perfectly. She seemed to spring off the ice when she jumped, and her spins were exceptional. In fact, she invented a unique combination of a flying camel spin and a sit spin that became known as the "Hamill Camel." Even though competition insecurity often plagued her, "Dot" always had the ability to perform under pressure.

"I was skating better than I had ever skated in my life ... and when I had finished I was the Olympic gold medalist."

DOROTHY HAMILL, 1983

Scott Hamilton

U.S.A.

Olympic Champion, 1984
World Champion, 1981-1984

Years after being crowned Olympic Champion, Scott Hamilton is still one of the most popular skaters in the world. His choreography is clever and humorous and it combines his speedy footwork with jumps that have quick rotation and smooth landings. Because of his consistency, Hamilton has topped many younger Olympic medalists in the tough world of professional men's competition.

"At my first two Nationals I came last. If there had been a space below last, I would have placed there. So never give up."

SCOTT HAMILTON, 1997

Ekaterina Gordeeva & Sergei Grinkov

Russia

Olympic Champions, 1988, 1994
World Champions, 1986, 1987, 1989, 1990

One of the greatest teams in pairs' history, Ekaterina Gordeeva and Sergei Grinkov had beautiful lifts, exciting throws and an ability to skate as one. But it was their love for each other and skating that really captivated their fans. Tragically, Grinkov died suddenly in 1995, but Gordeeva continues the pairs' magic on ice performing as a singles skater.

"It was magic when they were on the ice. They loved to skate, and because they felt joy, the audience felt joy."

MARINA ZUEVA, 1997
Gordeeva and Grinkov's coach

Best Pairs

Jenni Meno & Todd Sand

U.S.A.

U.S. National Champions, 1994-1996

Jenni Meno and Todd Sand's grace and unison, and the way they relate to each other, are tough to beat. Their lifts and pairs' moves are also excellent, and Meno's landings on throws are clean and flowing. If this elegant duo can consistently nail their tricks, they will have many years of success ahead of them.

Kyoko Ina & Jason Dungjen

U.S.A.

U.S. National Champions, 1997, 1998

The energetic style of this athletic team showcases their outstanding lifts and strong side-by-side jumps. Kyoko Ina and Jason Dungjen worked long and hard after placing second in their country for three years in a row. If their unison and ability to express emotion continue to improve, other victories will definitely be theirs.

Marina Eltsova & Andrei Bushkov

Russia

World Champions, 1996

Marina Eltsova wanted to be a ballet dancer while Andrei Bushkov dreamed of playing NHL hockey. Now, he uses his athletic ability to hoist Eltsova into awesome lifts, while she displays a dancer's graceful form. After they finished fourth in 1995, their coach told them to quit. Instead, they switched coaches and won Worlds the next year!

Oksana Kazakova & Artur Dmitriev

Russia

Olympic Champions, 1998
Olympic Champion, 1992
(Dmitriev & Natalia Mishkutenok)
World Champion, 1991, 1992
(Dmitriev & Mishkutenok)

Oksana Kazakova and Artur Dmitriev won the 1996 European title after skating together for only six months. Their skating combines speed, passion and grace with original choreography that highlights Kazakova's flexibility. When it counted most, this team skated brilliantly at the 1998 Olympics and captured gold.

Mandy Woetzel & Ingo Steuer

Germany

Olympic Bronze, 1998
World Champions, 1997

The road to the top has not been easy for Mandy Woetzel and Ingo Steuer. They have suffered agonizing injuries, yet they keep skating. This team is fast and has great side-by-side tricks. They are especially tough competitors, because they keep improving — they dazzle audiences with innovative programs every year.

Gold Medal Men

Elvis Stojko

Canada

Olympic Silver, 1994, 1998
World Champion, 1994, 1995, 1997

Often the climb to the top is easier than staying there. Elvis Stojko learned that in 1996 when his attempt at a "three-peat" as World Champion ended with a fall. But the most consistent and powerful jumper in the world never gave up, and he won again in 1997 after nailing a quad-toe, triple-toe combo — the first ever at Worlds. At the 1998 Olympics Stojko put out an incredible effort and skated with a severe injury to win the silver medal.

"The Olympics is a lot more than gold. It's about challenging yourself."

ELVIS STOJKO, 1998

Alexei Urmanov

Russia

Olympic Champion, 1994

Like all Soviet skaters, Alexei Urmanov used to have his expenses paid by his government. But since the breakup of the Soviet Union, paying for ice time as well as keeping in shape have been major challenges. Poor training conditions haven't stopped Urmanov from nailing triples and even a quad, however. He is sometimes criticized for his elaborate costumes, but claims they enhance his routines.

"After the short [program] I was thinking 'it's over for me' and now I sit here with the [European Championship] gold medal. I'm so lucky.

ALEXEI URMANOV, 1997

Todd Eldredge

U.S.A.

World Champion, 1996

Todd Eldredge skates fast and his tricks are smooth and effortless. He propels himself easily into huge jumps that travel far and wide across the ice. But skating hasn't always been easy for Eldredge. At one point, bad luck plagued him and he was so discouraged that he quit. But Eldredge soon returned to the ice with a new attitude — one that has taken him to the top.

"With the way things are going now, if you miss one element and the other guys do all their stuff, they're going to beat you."

TODD ELDREDGE, 1996

Ilia Kulik

Russia

Olympic Champion, 1998
World Junior Champion, 1995

At the age of 17, Ilia Kulik took the skating world by storm, winning the European Championships on his first try. Although his strength is smooth, classical-style skating, Kulik also spins and jumps with ease and can complete the quad-toe combo. He has battled with inconsistency at times, but he skated the performance of his life at the 1998 Olympics to win gold.

"I want to win everything, the Olympics too. I know I can do this."

ILIA KULIK, 1996

Superstar Ice Dancers

> *"We don't know how everything will happen, but we try to do everything for this [an Olympic medal]."*
>
> ANJELIKA KRYLOVA, 1996

Anjelika Krylova & Oleg Ovsiannikov

Russia

Olympic Silver, 1998
Russian Champions, 1995

In Russia, competition is fierce in ice dance, so when Anjelika Krylova and Oleg Ovsiannikov won the National title on their first try, they grabbed the spotlight. This elegant couple only began skating together in May 1994, but by 1996 they were silver medalists at Worlds. That's an extremely fast rise in ice dance. Krylova and Ovsiannikov have beautiful programs and their dance technique is excellent, but it's their smoothness and grace that especially delights audiences.

Shae-Lynn Bourne & Victor Kraatz

Canada

Canadian Champions, 1993-1998

Shae-Lynn Bourne and Victor Kraatz moved up the world ice dance standings amazingly fast — from 14th place to 3rd in just 4 years. That's because they improve constantly and each season introduce new and unusual ideas to their choreography, which also makes excellent use of the ice surface. Athletic yet elegant, Bourne and Kraatz skate on deep edges and use tremendous speed in their footwork and innovative moves.

"I love it when the crowd gets excited. We want to light up the crowd because it keeps us going and gives us energy."

SHAE-LYNN BOURNE, 1996

Pasha Grishuk & Evgeny Platov

Russia

Olympic Champions, 1994, 1998
World Champions, 1994-1996

Their style is unique, their speed is legendary, and they have nerves of steel. Pasha Grishuk and Evgeny Platov are seasoned performers who have competed so much that Platov claims a competition feels just like a practice session. They are masters of modern contemporary dance. With their win at the 1998 Olympics, Grishuk and Platov became the first ice dance team to win gold at two Olympic championships.

"It's our dream to get that second [Olympic] gold medal."

PASHA GRISHUK, 1997

43

Top Women

Michelle Kwan

U.S.A.

Olympic Silver, 1998
World Champion, 1996

At Worlds in 1995, 14-year-old Michelle Kwan outskated and outjumped her competitors, yet she only placed fourth. So she returned in 1996 with a more sophisticated program that emphasized her grace and beautiful moves, and earned a gold medal. Leading up to the 1998 Olympics, Kwan missed several weeks of training because of an injured foot. But she still managed to skate flawlessly and earn a silver medal. When she skates, Kwan wears a necklace with a dragon on it, which is a Chinese symbol of good luck.

"Michelle Kwan is a great role model. She works her brains out, never complains and never blames anyone else for her problems. She is self motivated and has an inner sense of what works on the ice."

FRANK CARROLL, 1997
Kwan's coach

Tara Lipinski

U.S.A.

Olympic Champion, 1998
World Champion, 1997

The years 1997 and 1998 belonged to Tara Lipinski after she became the youngest-ever champion at the 1997 Nationals and World Championships, and the 1998 Olympics. Full of energy with nerves of steel, "Leapin' Lipinski" is the first woman to land a triple-loop, triple-loop combination and she also nails all the other triple jumps easily. In the air she points her toes and crosses her legs and feet perfectly, which gives her quick rotation. Lipinski has superb spins and choreography that highlights her enthusiasm and her love of skating.

"I knew I was at the Olympics and skating [well]. I felt it was one of the best programs I'd ever done, technically and emotionally."

TARA LIPINSKI,
1998

Irina Slutskaia

Russia

World Junior Champion, 1995

Energetic and athletic, Irina Slutskaia is the first Russian woman ever to win the European Championships. She dreams of becoming a movie star but she's so talented on ice that she's already a skating star. As Slutskaia fearlessly bombs around the ice, she throws herself into powerful jumps. Her spins are amazing too. Slutskaia performs a variation of the back-breaking Biellmann spin (see page 30) that is even more difficult than the original: she spins on one foot, and then repeats it all on the other foot.

"My life has been devoted to skating. I'm not thinking about the money; that's not what counts for me."

IRINA SLUTSKAIA,
1996

Future Stars

Vanessa Gusmeroli

France

Vanessa Gusmeroli is an energetic skater with huge jumps. In the past she has had trouble with her consistency, but she put that behind her and skated to a bronze medal finish at the 1997 World Championships. Gusmeroli has a unique skating style and creative choreography. If she can continue to handle the pressure in competition, she'll stand on the winners' podium at future contests.

"The big thing for her is to improve artistically. She's an extremely high, explosive jumper and a promising skater."
ALAN SHRAMM, 1996 Gusmeroli's choreographer

Alexei Yagudin

Russia

World Junior Champion, 1996

Today, men's skating tends to be a contest of who can perform the best jumps, and Alexei Yagudin fits right in. He was only 16 at his first Worlds but he earned a bronze medal with a performance that rivaled the world's best. Yagudin learned a quad-toe jump in only one week — a remarkably short time. If he can improve his presentation and style, he will continue to be a threat in competition.

"It is time for him to transform to the next level, but most important that he be unique."
ALEXEI MISHIN, 1996 Yagudin's coach

Elena Berezhnaia & Anton Sikharulidze

Russia

Olympic Silver, 1998

After a horrible skating accident in which her partner's blade severely gashed her skull, Elena Berezhnaia required brain surgery. It almost ended her career, but in less than a year she was skating with her new partner, Anton Sikharulidze. Berezhnaia and Sikharulidze could be the world's best pair one day, because they have it all: speed, power, unison and grace.

"This team has the potential and quality of skating that could make them dominate pairs' skating for years, if they can learn to handle the pressure of competition."

BARBARA UNDERHILL, 1997 World Pairs' Champion

"We dream, of course, to be the best one day."

ILIA AVERBUKH, 1997

Irina Lobacheva & Ilia Averbukh

Russia

Russian Champions, 1997

Ice dancers Irina Lobacheva and Ilia Averbukh are exciting and daring, and their innovative routines are jam-packed with difficult moves. They jumped an incredible nine spots in the World ice dance standings, from 15th in 1995 to 6th in 1996, and beat the heavyweights of Russian dance when they won Nationals in 1997. If they can further develop their unique style, Lobacheva and Averbukh will enjoy many years of success.

Index